The Search Fo
Constable's Rain

The Search For Constable's Rainbow
A Snowy Owl Art Story

Paperback ISBN-13: 978-1-60571-627-5

SHIRES●PRESS
Manchester Center, Vermont

Available on Amazon

Other books by D. Sunda and D. Wraga are *The Panda Bear That Saved The Zoo, Letters From The Animals, Puppy Quincy Loves Hats, The Owl That Saved The Christmas Tree Forest,* and *Snowy Owl and the Musical Echo.* Watch for more Snowy Owl stories.

The Search For Constable's Rainbows

A Snowy Owl
Art Story

With the flip of an ear and the blink of an eye, Puppy Quincy's inner clock told him it was time to join his friends Chloe, Top Hat and Jelly Bean. Chloe is the neighbour's adorable basset hound puppy. Top Hat the horse is Puppy Quincy's long-standing friend, and Jelly Bean is his newest friend, a pony that can jump over just about everything.

It was a school day for Matilda, Jonnie, Matthew and Naomi. On school days, the animal friends loved waiting for the children at their school gates to follow them home.

How they loved listening to the children talk about their day in school! The children had an art project due before tomorrow's museum trip. They reminded each other that they must remember to include all the colours of a rainbow in their design: violet, indigo, blue, green, yellow, orange and red.

Excitedly, Matthew said: "I have a great idea for a design. There are four of us, and as we have been learning about how rainbows appear in the sky, let's design a rare quadruple rainbow." All four immediately clapped their hands as it was a brilliant idea. Naomi noted that they had learned that rainbows are really circles. We only see an arc because we don't see the part of the rainbow below the horizon. "So," she said, "the design could show the colours in the shape of a circle. Or we could also design a rainbow fan." The others instantly exclaimed: "A fan would be fun!"

The children began working together on their project. While they enjoyed the hot chocolate and chocolate cookies that Mrs. Howland, Matilda and Jonnie's mother, had made, Mrs. Howland explained how rainbows are formed. She described how the reflection of light appears through the rain droplets. She added that she once saw a red sunset rainbow, one of the rarest of all rainbow formations, as most rainbows appear in the late morning or in the afternoon.

This was an exciting week for the children. The special museum trip tomorrow was a visit to the art museum. The children couldn't wait to view the exhibition of paintings by John Constable. He included rainbows in some of the paintings, so their art teacher had shared her knowledge of the painter's understanding of science, especially meteorology and the creation of rainbows. Puppy Quincy and his friends, including the magical Snowy Owl, were as excited as the children.

The special museum trip day arrived. With packed lunch boxes, the children walked to the meeting point at the local museum. Puppy Quincy and his friends followed. When the art tour commenced, the animal friends were sad to have to wait outside. However, thanks to Snowy Owl, they had a secret plan. Snowy pointed them to the large museum windows which would allow them all to watch the children studying the spectacular paintings by Constable. Many showed enormous landscapes, Constable's favourite local buildings, his unsurpassed cloud and sky formations and, indeed, his inclusion of rainbows.

After thanking Snowy for his usual brilliant plan, the four animal friends crowded together to look through the very tall museum windows. They couldn't believe their eyes! The paintings were so breathtaking! All the paintings they could see were beyond belief, and many of the scenes included rainbows.

"How I do love Constable's rainbows!" exclaimed Puppy Quincy. "They are so beautiful and look so real." He kept repeating, "I love his rainbows. I just love them!" Chloe, Top Hat and Jelly Bean all understood his excited puppy chatter. They all joined in, chanting "Rainbows, rainbows! We must find a real rainbow," each in its own special way: barks and howls from Puppy Quincy and Chloe, neighs from Top Hat and Jelly Bean and hoots from Snowy.

Suddenly, all the school children poured out of the museum building, carrying their lunch boxes to find the welcoming picnic tables. They settled at the tables to eat lunch and chattered about all they had seen. No one had noticed the distant rain clouds that were just beginning to clear. Chloe looked up to the sky. Because she was so alert, she was the first to see a beautiful rainbow! Her howl was such a sweet attention getter that all the children and animals looked at her. Jelly Bean saw the rainbow next and instinctively jumped back and forth over the tall yew hedge to support Chloe's attempt to tell all to look up at the rainbow. Respectfully, Top Hat bowed to Chloe and then to Jelly Bean to share his wholehearted thanks and that of Puppy Quincy as well. Snowy Owl fluttered above them, as entranced by the rainbow as the others.

As everyone, animals and children alike, gazed at the rainbow, commenting that it looked exactly like Constable's rainbows, they were interrupted by the voice of their art teacher. "Why do you think that Constable included rainbows, including a double rainbow, in some of his paintings?"

Matthew answered first. "I think he knew a lot about science, especially how rainbows are formed."

Naomi shared: "John Constable loved colour. He knew how to expertly weave colour into his scenes. He understood light."

Jonnie piped up: "I think that Constable suggests that rainbows are magical. Each of us could make a wish!"

"He gives us hope and the promise of beauty in all we see," added Matilda.

Then all the children exclaimed: "Let's make a wish!"

When all had made a wish, Puppy Quincy and his friends looked at each other, secretly wondering what each had wished for. The children had noticed that Puppy Quincy was wearing his Snowy River hat. Top Hat was, as always, wearing his winning top hat, and Chloe was wearing a floppy sun hat given to her by her neighbours, who loved her to bits. But Jelly Bean had no hat yet.

The school children made a special hat for Jelly Bean. It was a hat that allowed his ears to show and his character to shine. They had painted the hat with jelly beans in all the colours of the rainbow. As the hat was placed on Jelly Bean's head, four truly stunning rainbows appeared overhead! As all the children and the animal friends stared at this most rare and magical view, Puppy Quincy was reminded of his team of four friends with Snowy Owl looking over them like a lucky star. And he thought of the four wonderful children whom they all adored.

Everyone's wishes had come true – true violet, true indigo, true blue, true green, true yellow, true orange and true red. Jelly Bean showed her thanks by jumping the hedge back and forth four times! Chloe performed her musical howl, and Top Hat bowed in every direction.

Puppy Quincy led his friends and the children home with a trot and a joyful prance. Snowy Owl flew along with them.

Much later, as the sun was setting, the four animal friends gathered together, remembering their very special day. Just as earlier in the day, there had been dark clouds in the distance. It had been an interesting weather day, thought Puppy Quincy: sun and clouds and rain and rainbows. He said to his friends in his barking puppy language: "I think Constable would have loved a day like this!" Chloe, Top Hat and Jelly Bean agreed. Snowy Owl hooted his agreement from the tree branch where he perched.

The sun was setting, and the sunset sky was fading. Suddenly, Chloe began to howl while looking up at the sky. Her friends looked up and saw one more rainbow – a very rare red sunset rainbow, just as Mrs. Howland had described! Puppy Quincy said: "I wonder if John Constable ever saw a sunset rainbow. It would be such a beautiful painting!" Chloe wondered if anyone had wished to see a sunset rainbow earlier, when all were making wishes.

Puppy Quincy, Chloe, Top Hat, Jelly Bean and Snowy Owl barked, howled, neighed and hooted to call Matthew, Naomi, Matilda and Jonnie to come out and see the very special rainbow. As all gathered outside, a shooting star streaked across the darkening sky, and the rainbow faded. It had truly been a magical day! Through art and the rainbows, they had all learned so much: to appreciate the beauty around them, to feel the power of art and to share all the joys of friendship. This was a lesson they would remember today, tomorrow and forever more!

The Snowy Owl Team Credits:

Debbi Wraga
Publisher & International Creative Art Director
(childrensbooksbeloved.com)

Dianne Sunda
Author & Co-Designer

Diane Macris
Co-Author

Georgia Hamp
Illustrator & Co-Designer

Kelly Benoit
Creative Arts Fellow
(internationalchildrensmuseumfoundation.com)